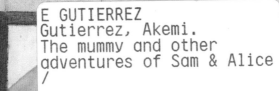

The Mummy
AND OTHER ADVENTURES OF
Sam & Alice

by Akemi Gutierrez

Houghton Mifflin Company
Boston 2005

www.houghtonmifflinbooks.com

The text of this book is set in Sassoon.
The illustrations are gouache on watercolor paper.

Library of Congress Cataloging-in-Publication Data
Gutierrez, Akemi.
The mummy and other adventures of Sam & Alice / by Akemi Gutierrez.
p. cm.
Summary: Sam and his little sister Alice have fun playing together.
ISBN 0-618-50761-2
[1. Brothers and sisters—Fiction. 2. Play—Fiction.] I. Title.
PZ7.G9842Mu 2005
[E]—dc22
2004013203

ISBN-13: 978-0618-50761-0

Manufactured in China
SCP 10 9 8 7 6 5 4 3 2 1

For Joyce and Alison. And our brothers, Wayne, Mike, and Glenn.

Contents

What's in Sam's Sock?

Sam and Alice were walking to the park.

"Oww," said Sam. "There's something in my sock."
"I bet it's nothing but a little teeny pebble," said Alice.

"No, it's bigger than a pebble," said Sam.
"What if a baby mouse crawled into your sock?"
asked Alice.

"I would love to have a baby mouse!"

"There isn't a baby mouse in my sock," said Sam.
"I think it's a skateboard."

"Maybe there are bunnies in your sock instead?"
asked Alice.

"Absolutely no bunnies are in my sock," said Sam.
"It's a robot."

"Or a rhinoceros," said Alice quietly.

"Nope," said Sam. "I'm sure it's a dragon."

"But couldn't a sea lion have slipped into your sock?"
asked Alice.

"No, it's bigger than a sea lion," replied Sam.
"I bet it's a spaceship."

"I think a tiger took a nap in your sock," said Alice.

"No tiger. It's definitely a train," answered Sam.

"I hope it's a bear!" Alice giggled.

"I don't want a dumb bear in my sock," Sam said.
"I'm sure it's a pirate ship!"

"But I want a bear." Alice pouted.

"Then get your own sock," said Sam.

And he pulled his sock off and shook it until out popped . . .

"It's nothing but a little teeny pebble!" cried Alice.

"Yeah," said Sam. "But it could have been an airplane."

"Yes, it could have been," Alice said, smiling.
"I like planes."

The Jungle

Sam and Alice were exploring the scariest jungle in the world.

"Be careful," whispered Sam. "There's danger everywhere."

Just then, a big, mean Swamp Rat jumped out of the bushes.

The Swamp Rat grabbed Sam in its greasy paws and was about to gobble him up, shoes and all, when . . .

Alice shouted, "My brother is not a piece of cheese!" And
she gave that Swamp Rat such a pinch that it squeaked
a loud "EEEK," dropped Sam, and ran away.

"That was close," said Sam. "The river will be safer.
Follow me."

So Sam and Alice paddled downstream on the dark and winding water.

Suddenly, a Sea Monster rose out of the river and
grabbed Alice in its slimy flippers. It was about to
swallow her whole, shoes and all, when . . .

Sam shouted, "My sister is not a fish stick!" And he gave that Sea Monster such a pinch that it gurgled a loud "BLUG-BLUG-BLAARG," dropped Alice, and swam away.

"Let's climb to higher ground," said Sam.

But as soon as they reached the top of the mountain, a hungry Cave Bat swooped down and grabbed Sam in its hairy claws. It was about to carry him off, shoes and all, when . . .

Alice didn't do anything.

"HELP ME!" Sam yelled.
"Nope," said Alice calmly.
"WHY NOT?!" shouted Sam.

"Lunchtime!" Alice said, smiling.

"I thought I was a goner," said Sam.
"Not before lunch," laughed Alice.

The Mummy

Sam was in the backyard sandbox.
"What are you making?" asked Alice.

"Pyramid," replied Sam. "In Egypt, there are pyramids and inside them are mummies and treasure."

Alice started to make something in the sandbox, too.
"What's that?" asked Sam.
"It's a mummy," said Alice.

"Oh yeah?" Sam laughed. "I bet if you saw a REAL mummy, you'd be scared to bits."

"I wouldn't be scared," Alice said.
"I would play games with him."

"Games?" asked Sam. "Wouldn't you want to travel to Egypt with him?"

"We would go to the park," said Alice.

"But he could reveal the secrets of the pyramids!" cried Sam.

"We would enjoy some sunshine," said Alice.

"Don't you want to know where the treasures are hidden?" asked Sam.

"We would walk the dog," said Alice.

"Aren't you interested in learning his language?" asked Sam.

"We would have ice cream, because mummies really like sweets," Alice said.

"Do little sisters like sweets, too?" asked Sam.

"We sure do!" said Alice.

The End